Praise for Anne Charnock's
A Calculated Life

Shortlisted for the 2013 Philip K. Dick and
Kitschies Golden Tentacle Awards

"Charnock is a subtle world builder . . . for readers who want a smart, subtle exploration of human emotion and intelligence, this is an excellent choice." —Alix E. Harrow, *Strange Horizons*

"Charnock has fascinating, complex things to say about work, sex, family and hope . . . What she shares with (Philip K.) Dick is the ability to write unease . . . a very noteworthy book." —Adam Roberts, author of *Jack Glass*, winner of the 2012 BSFA Best Novel Award

"This is a story beautifully and simply narrated, the language economical but evocative, and it remains compelling without ever resorting to sensationalism. A coming-of-age tale exploring what it means to be human, it kept me gripped to the end." —E. J. Swift, author of The Osiris Project trilogy

"This story puts us inside one of the most interesting perspectives I've encountered in recent fiction. Jayna's perspective is so unique that I would happily have followed her anywhere, and, as a consequence, the cleverness of this plot almost snuck up on me. A smart, stylish, emotionally compelling book with literary richness and sci-fi smarts." —Susan DeFreitas, author of *Pyrophitic*

"Gets the grey matter firing . . . Such easily accessible yet intelligent fiction can be quite a rarity, and one to be savored." —*The Taichung Bookworm*

"There is a degree of elegance in the uncluttered prose that Charnock wields to introduce optimism into a pessimistic view of the future." —*Tzer Island*

"Charnock [being] an astute observer herself, what results is an inquiry into feminism and society that will make the reader truly pause to compare their own experiences and perceptions." —*Speculiction*

"*A Calculated Life*, by Anne Charnock, is one of those books that while overtly science fiction is really a great insight into humanity today. Ultimately . . . this book is more about human emotion and intelligence than it is about the future: And it's that exploration that makes this such a compelling work." —*Geek in Sydney*